/
K499g

GANZY
REMEMBERS

ATHENEUM
Macmillan Publishing Company
866 Third Avenue, New York, NY 10022

Collier Macmillan Canada, Inc.
1200 Eglinton Avenue East
Suite 200
Don Mills, Ontario M3C 3N1

First Edition
Printed in Singapore
10   9   8   7   6   5   4   3   2   1

Library of Congress Cataloging-in-Publication Data
Ketner, Mary Grace.
Ganzy remembers/Mary Grace Ketner; illustrated by Barbara
Sparks. — 1st ed.
p.   cm.
Summary: Ganzy tells her daughter, granddaughter, and great-
granddaughter stories about her childhood on a Texas farm years ago.
ISBN 0–689–31610–0
[1. Great-grandmothers—Fiction.   2. Farm life—Texas—Fiction.
3. Texas—Fiction.]   I. Sparks, Barbara, ill.   II. Title.
PZ7.K4895Gam   1991
[E]—dc20
89–78261   CIP   AC

GANZY
REMEMBERS

by Mary Grace Ketner

illustrated by Barbara Sparks

ATHENEUM 1991 NEW YORK

COLLIER MACMILLAN CANADA

TORONTO

MAXWELL MACMILLAN INTERNATIONAL PUBLISHING GROUP

NEW YORK   OXFORD   SINGAPORE   SYDNEY

To Kate, Virginia
and, of course, Daphne
——M. G. K.

For my mother and father
——B. S.

Sometimes Grandmother and I go to see my great-grandmother in the nursing home.

Grandmother calls her "Mama." Mother and I say "Ganzy," and so do all my aunts and uncles and cousins. The nurses call her "Mrs. Heidel." When she was a little girl, everyone called her "Daphne."

Her eyes are gray now, and her hair is silver. When she was a
little girl, she had shiny dark eyes and long brown hair with bangs.

Ganzy sleeps during much of the day, but when she was
Daphne she didn't. She got up before sunrise and went out to play
with the goats. They played King of the Mountain.

Then she would feed Hunsie and Dunie, the twin baby lambs
that Uncle George had given her.

The nurse brings Ganzy her lunch, and Grandmother helps her eat it. Ganzy remembers how she used to help her mother make lunch in the morning. Every day it was bacon and biscuits. Bacon and biscuits every day. She carried it to school in a bucket.

Grandmother and I push Ganzy to the garden in her wheelchair. She remembers riding her horse, Prince, to school.

They always went the same way: across Lamb Creek, around the mountain, and past Uncle Ben's house through the big field where the bluebonnets bloom every spring.

A breeze comes over the garden wall, so Grandmother and I pull
Ganzy's shawl around her shoulders for her.

Ganzy remembers a winter morning so cold that she stopped
Prince in a clearing and hopped down to build a little fire to warm
herself before going on to school.

"Hello, Vera. How are you today, Amos?" Grandmother says to
Ganzy's friends as we walk.

Ganzy remembers that her school friends used to wait for her at the beginning of the path through the woods, and they would all go the rest of the way together.

One of her friends rode an old mule to school. Every day at ten o'clock, the mule would bray. No one knew why. The children read and recited and ciphered. When it got close to ten o'clock, they'd begin to listen for him. Sure enough: "Hee-haw, hee-haw, hee-haw."

Every day Daphne tried not to laugh, but when the mule started braying, someone would start giggling, then someone else, then Daphne or another child, until the whole class was laughing.

"Hee-haw, hee-haw, hee-haw."

Well, not the teacher.

Daphne liked school, and she especially liked to read. Her favorite book was *Caesar's Gallic Wars*.

I hold the door open and Grandmother pushes Ganzy back inside.

Ganzy remembers when she was Daphne, riding home after school.

She rode fast as lightning, fast as anything!

Uncle Ben watched Daphne race Prince across the field. He telephoned her mother.

"Ella," he said, "you're going to have to do something about that girl of yours! She's riding that horse too fast. She's going to get hurt one of these days!"

"Daphne," said her mother when she got home. "Don't ride so fast! Or at least, slow down when you go past Uncle Ben's!"

When we get back to Ganzy's room, we see that a repairman has come.

Ganzy remembers when she was Daphne. Sometimes when she got home, there would be someone she had never seen before sitting on the front porch. Her mother always invited travelers to stay over.

Once it was a man who was very sick. They nursed him back
to health and taught him to walk again. Then he moved on.

One time it was the bandit Pancho Villa. Mother and Papoo
didn't call him by name, but Daphne knew who he was. She had
heard other travelers tell stories about him.

Another time it was a trader playing checkers with her father.
Beside them on the porch, baby Fred cooed and sang and played
with a doll.

"That's a fine boy," said the trader. "What'll you take for 'im?"

"Oh, 'bout two bits," answered Papoo.

When it came time for supper, Daphne and Fred were nowhere
to be found.

"We wouldn't really sell your brother," said Papoo when he finally found them. He hugged Daphne closely.

Then baby Fred started crying and stamping his feet, and Daphne wished the trader would offer to buy him again.

The repairman likes Ganzy's stories, too. He laughs and shakes his screwdriver in the air. "That's a good one," he says.

Ganzy remembers that Papoo fixed everything around their house. Once he needed to repair the barbed-wire fence.

"Daphne, run fetch my overalls for me, please," he asked.

Daphne ran out to the clothesline where the overalls hung when they weren't being used. Soon she was back, but without the overalls.

"Where are they?" asked Papoo.

Daphne didn't answer. She looked very sad.

"Never mind! I'll get them myself," he said.

Daphne followed Papoo out to the clothesline. A sparrow had made a nest in his pocket.

"Peep, peep!" her babies called out.

"Well, Mama Bird!" said Papoo. "Do you think you need a home more than I need my overalls?"

The mama bird chirped at him from the clothesline pole.

"I s'pose you do."

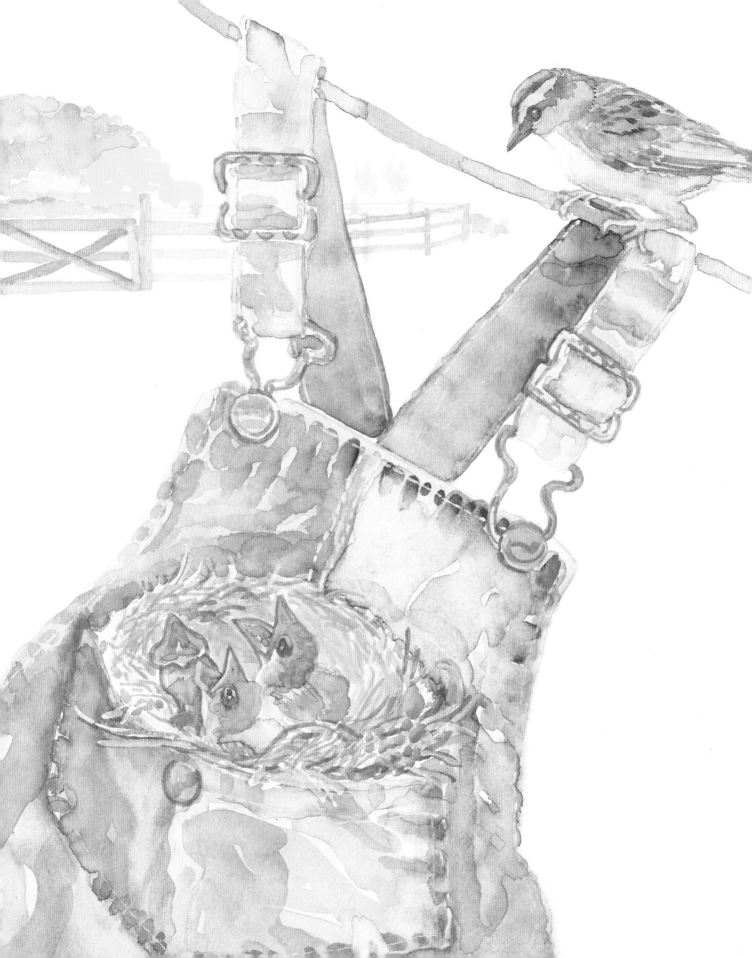

We push Ganzy to the mirror. Grandmother brushes her hair, and I draw a picture for her. Ganzy remembers.

In the evening, Daphne took a bath in the washtub or bathed with her mother in the creek.

When they bathed in the creek, she could practice her spelling words by writing them on the sandbar with a stick.

We push Ganzy back to her bed. The repairman helps us lift her into it. Grandmother talks with him a minute, and Ganzy talks to me. She remembers.

If travelers were camping in the field for the night, Daphne would sit at the campfire and listen to the grown-ups talk about what had been happening in their home counties.

If Aunt Lucy were visiting, she read Daphne bedtime stories that she wrote herself. Aunt Lucy's stories were good for putting people to sleep.

Now Ganzy doesn't need bedtime stories to go to sleep.
We whisper, "Good-bye," and tiptoe out.

We walk quietly down the hall to the door.

"Ganzy remembers lots of interesting things, doesn't she, Grandmother?" I say as we walk down the steps.

"Yes," says my grandmother. "And some of them really happened."